A
BEASTY
STORY

A BEASTY STORY

HUFF
PUFF
HUFF
PUFF
HUFF
PUFF
HUFF
PUFF
HUFF
PUFF

SNIPPETY
SNICK
SNIPPETY
SNICK
SNIPPETY
SNICK

NICK 5

HANK 6

Bill Martin Jr & Steven Kellogg

VOYAGER BOOKS · HARCOURT, INC.

San Diego   New York   London

Original text copyright © 1970 by Harcourt, Inc./Copyright renewed 1998 by Bill Martin Jr

This edition: Text copyright © 1999 by Bill Martin Jr and Steven Kellogg/Illustrations copyright © 1999 by Steven Kellogg

www.HarcourtBooks.com

First Voyager Books edition 2002

Voyager Books is a trademark of Harcourt, Inc., registered in the United States of America and/or other jurisdictions.

The Library of Congress has cataloged the hardcover edition as follows: Martin, Bill, 1916–   A beasty story/by Bill Martin Jr and Steven Kellogg; illustrated by Steven Kellogg.   p.   cm.

Summary: A group of mice venture into a dark, dark wood where they find a dark brown house with a dark red stair leading past other dark colors to a spooky surprise.

[1. Mice—Fiction. 2. Color—Fiction. 3. Stories in rhyme.] I. Kellogg, Steven, ill. II. Title.

PZ8.3.M3988Be 1999   [E]—dc21   97-49519   ISBN 0-15-201683-X   ISBN 0-15-216560-6 pb   B C D E F G H

This way to the dark DARK WOOD

Don't go.

With love and appreciation
to Michael Sampson and his family
—B. M. & S. K.

In a dark, dark wood there is a dark, dark house.

In the dark brown house there is a dark, dark stair.

here is a dark, dark cellar.

here is a dark, dark cupboard.

here is a dark, dark bottle.

the dark green bottle.

A BEAST!

It floats out of the dark green bottle.

through the dark purple cupboard,

up the dark red stair,

oward an even **DARKER** house,

and GRABS HIM!

There is a flash of light!

sounds of beasty laughter,

followed by beasty snores.

The first collaboration between two beloved creators of children's books!

BILL MARTIN JR is known worldwide for his classic picture books, including *Brown Bear, Brown Bear, What Do You See?* and *Polar Bear, Polar Bear, What Do You Hear?*, both illustrated by Eric Carle, and *Chicka Chicka Boom Boom*, illustrated by Lois Ehlert. Mr. Martin lives in Texas.

STEVEN KELLOGG has illustrated more than a hundred dearly loved books for children, including *A Hunting We Will Go!* and his own versions of the ever-popular tall tales *Johnny Appleseed*, *Pecos Bill*, and *Paul Bunyan*. Mr. Kellogg lives in Connecticut.